Friends Again

#JustFriends Series - Book 4

MARIE COLE

For my fans: past, present & future.

Friends Again

Chapter 1

"Hey, Kelly. I was wondering if you could pull up the budget for the Stroke of Midnight Gala." I leaned against her desk, careful not to wrinkle my brand new Valentino dress. I smiled sugary sweet as she grabbed the paper from the printer and held it out towards my waiting hand. "Thanks so much," I said.

"Oh, Jen!" she exclaimed, her body leaning forward as if she were about to divulge a secret. I was all about secrets. I raised my eyebrows and took the bait, leaning towards her too. "Have you seen the new doctor?" She was talking in a hushed voice, so soft it took me a few seconds to register what she'd said.

I glanced around, everyone else was out to lunch. "The balding man with the 'stache?" I wrinkled my nose in disgust as I thought about the man I'd had to share the elevator with last week. He'd smelled of stale smoke and fake cheese.

"No, no. That's Doctor Thomas. No. The new doctor is young…" I leaned forward a little more, intrigued. "And hot…" She had my full attention now. A new young, hot doctor? How had I missed him? And when could I meet him? Shacking up with a new doctor could be just what I needed to get the still bitter taste of divorce out of my mouth. As long as it was a one-time thing I could probably get away with it - even with the no fraternization policy in place.

"When did he start?"

"According to his HR forms, about two months ago but he's been slowly transitioning. His office is still pretty bare. Only a few dozen boxes, all packed."

"Then how do you know about him?"

"He had to come in to fill out forms for his compensation." She grinned like a cat with a mouse between its paws. It didn't say much. Kelly didn't exactly have the highest of standards.

"Is he single?"

"According to his HR forms and his lips when I asked him, the rumor is yes. I thought since you're now single that maybe…" she waggled her eyebrows and that was my cue to shut her down. I didn't need her or anyone else's pity.

I laughed to humor her and waved a limp hand in her direction. "Kelly, honestly. I'm fine."

Her brows perked up, eager for more office gossip. "So you're seeing someone?"

I nodded. Lying to this woman was not my biggest sin. "Oh yes. A woman like me doesn't stay single for long." Not when I have a rich daddy and a rich ex-husband paying me lots of alimony to stay far away from him and his new bride.

Kent.

Just thinking about him made my blood boil. I'd wasted fifteen years of my life on that man and how had he repaid me? With divorce papers and a serious complex. I knew he loved Elly, I knew it from the beginning but he'd always insisted it was innocent between them and that he didn't feel that way for her. Stupid me, I believed him. My mother was the only one who had understood and comforted me after the divorce. She too was victim to a self-serving marriage. I was beginning to wonder if true love was even possible.

"Well, good on you." She had the fakest smile plastered on her face. I knew it was fake because it was the same one I'd practiced in the mirror plenty of times in my life. When my first love left me. When my parents divorced. Every time Kent insisted he didn't have feelings for his now wife. When Kent divorced me. I pushed all that aside and put my fake smile on too.

"Good on me. Anyway, thanks for this. I'll see you later." As I pushed off her desk and started towards the elevators, I glanced at my phone and shook my head. "Dammit," I muttered as I picked up the pace in my black Manolo Blahnik high heeled knee boots. If I was late coming back from lunch with my mom my father was going to have my head and probably fire me from this job. This job was everything to me. The only thing really holding me together since my world fell apart.

I was cutting around the corner when someone crashed into me. A male someone. I gasped and held my arms out to the side helplessly as I felt hot wetness drench the front of my dress. The coffee burned, but not as much as the disdain I had for whomever had just ruined my dress. I was so livid I didn't even take a moment to look at him.

"You… asshole!" I moaned softly as I assessed the damage to my dress. "Goddamnit!" Without another word I quickly left him standing in the hall and retreated to the nearest bathroom. My heels echoed on the tile floor as I made quick work of grabbing up a handful of paper towels and wetting them. I looked down as I quickly blotted at the front of my dress. "Fucking Valentino coffee dress now. Damnit." When I looked up I saw him standing behind me, a serious expression on his face.

"I'm sorry. I didn't mean to ruin your dress." The rich timbre of his voice echoed throughout the tiled room.

I was struck motionless by the man I saw in the mirror who towered in the doorway, probably a few inches over six-feet. He looked so very familiar with his dark hair, his bronze-colored skin and dark amused eyes. My mind struggled to place him even as something in my chest was squeezing tightly. I hadn't had such a reaction to someone from the opposite sex since… No. Dominic was gone. I looked down as I unstuck myself, dabbing the dress, anything so I didn't have to look in that man's eyes. They were bringing up feelings I had struggled to push away since I was fourteen.

"Wow. You've changed since the last time I saw you."

Since the last time…? My head shot up and I met his gaze again. Part of me wanted it to be true. Could this be the boy who left me without even the kindness of a goodbye?

Chapter 2

I tossed the wet paper towel into the trash and turned to face him. With clenched fists I lifted my chin and gave my blonde hair a gentle toss. "Should I know who you are?"

His deep brown eyes didn't widen in shock as I'd expected, instead they crinkled as his lips widened into a smile. "I would hope so. But it was many years ago and I have filled out a bit since then. Grown up. Made something of myself."

My heart was beating wildly in my chest at the thought of this man being my Dominic. I swallowed back more bitterness. Even if this was him, he wasn't my Dominic. He never had been. He'd just been the boy who'd stolen my innocence and made me believe he loved me. Just as Kent hadn't ever been my Kent. He'd always been Elly's Kent. At least where it mattered.

"Jen, amor de mi vida," he said, his voice low and soft, the past rushing over me as he whispered those words.

I held up my hand and shook my head. "No. I'm sorry. I can't do this." I stepped around him and was out the door before my heart made me do something stupid.

I listened intently for footsteps behind me but I heard nothing. I was partially relieved and partially disappointed. It felt good to walk out on him just like he'd done to me. An eye for an eye, both without a goodbye.

I needed to get home and change before the big meeting with my father. On the way I called my mother and cancelled our lunch. She was disappointed but she understood. His name was on the tip of my lips. There was no one else I trusted more than my mother. But I couldn't tell her. Not yet. There was nothing to tell. Yet.

I rushed back to the office with ten minutes to spare. This left me sitting in the chair in the hallway in front of my father's office with nothing to do. I sighed heavily as I looked down at the papers in my lap. I had planned a lot already, I could only hope my father would approve everything. Not that I minded starting over, I'd had lots of practice with that. But I'd worked so hard on this and my vision for this gala, my first real event here planned and executed all by myself, was crystal clear.

When I heard the door to my father's office open I glanced up. I felt the scowl on my face as Dominic stepped out of the office, my father's hand patting him on the back.

"I'm so glad you're finally here, son. You'll be a wonderful asset to the team. Don't forget that if you need anything at all to find Kelly, she will show you the ropes around here."

The smile on my father's face looked so genuine. I felt a twisting in my gut that I realized was something like jealousy. I was turning my eyes away when my father caught and held them.

"Ah, Jen. I'm glad you're on time, sweetheart." I felt the passive aggressive jab. I stood up and smiled. He was the one man who was always unrattled by my outbursts. He didn't give in. He wasn't affected. It always left me wondering if he felt anything at all. But now, seeing a real smile on his face, reserved for Dominic, it was obvious he just didn't feel anything at all for me, his only child. "Guess who I found while at a conference in Atlanta?" I raised my eyebrows, as if I had no idea. "Dominic Santos. You do remember him, don't you? You two used to play together."

It was my turn to smile genuinely now. We played together alright. We played together very often while my dad was off doing whatever he was doing with whoever and my mother was off self-medicating with excessive exercise and spa treatments. My eyes moved over Dominic again, starting with his deep sea Berluti loafers, light gray pants -they definitely appeared to be designer-, and a checkered shirt that was hidden underneath a very nice fitting crewneck sweater. If I was a sucker for anything it was a well-dressed man. I kept my smile steady as I nodded, even though my heart was once again beating wildly. The last thing my eyes spotted was a tiny 'J' on his wrist. There was no longer any doubt about his identity. It was him.

One afternoon I told him that if he really loved me he'd prove it. He'd asked me how and I'd responded that he'd brand himself, like those bad boys in the movies. A tattoo with my name. He'd only gotten the J done with the gas burner, a paperclip and black pen ink before his mother had walked in.

He was staring at me, waiting for our gazes to meet. He was smiling, as if he read my thoughts and was imagining the two of us in the throes of lust and hormones. "I remember, Dr. Derby." Daddy had lots of rules. One of them was to address him formally whenever we were in public.

Dominic stretched out his hand. I considered for a moment not accepting it but I did anyway. I had to know if the lust between us was still there after all these years. And that had been a mistake. As soon as our hands touched my body reacted. I felt the tingle on my palm which immediately seared up my arm. "Great to see you again, Jen. Perhaps we can get dinner sometime and catch up? I'm sure we have a lot to tell each other."

I pulled my hand from his and was about to open my mouth to shut him down when my father spoke up. "Oh, that's a wonderful idea! Jen would be more than happy to have dinner with you, wouldn't you, sweetheart?"

I cleared my throat and nodded politely. It was what was expected of me. And where my father was concerned I always did what was expected of me. I couldn't shake six-year-old Jen who always stood at the door waiting for her daddy to come home so she could give him a hug.

"Yes, that would be great," I replied, my words robotic to my own ears.

"Wonderful, wonderful. Alright, Dr. Santos, I'll get back to you about that date."

Dominic turned his attention back to my father and with a nod he started to walk away. He paused and turned back, his deep brown eyes heating my body with just a look. "Jen, how will I reach you?"

I wanted to tell him to go to hell. I didn't want to react this way to him. Not him. Damn my traitorous body.

"Go talk to Kelly. She has Jen's contact information." He winked at Dominic before moving between us. He put his hand on my back and ushered me into his office. "I have five minutes before my next meeting, Jen. What do you need?"

All those tingly feelings disappeared at once and my brain stuttered momentarily. "We had a meeting today to discuss the gala."

My father sighed as he leaned back against his desk, his hands cupped the edge of the wood on either side of him. "Oh right, the gala. I had to move your meeting to next week. Didn't Rachel tell you?" Rachel was daddy's secretary. She was pretty but that was about all she had going for her.

"No, she didn't." I licked my lips and quickly pulled out my notes. "Just look at it really quickly, daddy, and let me know if-"

"Jen, we've talked about this."

I paused and glanced up, meeting his angry gaze. I shook my head and furrowed my brows. "I'm sorry. Dr. Derby, please take a look at this and let me know if I'm on the right track with your vision."

He snatched the paper and looked it over quickly before he held it back out. "It looks fine, Jen. You know I'm not one for party planning. That was always your mother's thing. Look, I'm going to give this to Dr. Santos. He's new and doesn't have many patients yet. I'm giving him the authority to approve or disapprove the details of the gala."

I nodded as I tucked the paper back into its folder. I kept my eyes down, suddenly feeling as if my whole world were being tilted on its axis. I was going to have to work with him. "Okay, thank you."

There was a knock on the door which signaled to my father that his next appointment, the one more important than his own daughter, was here. When the door opened my father pointed to his secretary, "Rachel, please send Dr. Santos a message to let him know he'll be handling the gala with Jen."

I smiled as I moved out into the hallway and tried not to let the disappointment show on my face. My father was a very important man and he had a lot on his plate. I shouldn't have expected things would change just because he'd found a place for me at his medical firm.

I was on my way to the elevator when I felt my phone vibrating in my Coach bag. I pushed the button to call the elevator and then stepped back, fishing my phone from my purse.

DOMINIC: I KNOW IT'S PROBABLY A LONG SHOT, BUT ARE YOU FREE FOR DINNER TONIGHT?

I shook my head and stuffed my phone back into my bag.

"You're not even going to answer my text?" I jumped at the sound of his voice. He was coming towards me, a too-handsome smile on his face. Did he already hear the news? I looked away, I wasn't going to let him get under my skin and into my heart. Not again.

Chapter 3

I chose to ignore him as I stepped onto the elevator. I tried to push the 'door close' button before he could climb in, but he was quicker and slipped into the elevator just as the doors began to shut. I rolled my eyes as he stood too close to me. I could feel the heat from his body and smell the fragrance that clung to his clothes.

"Come on, Jen. I get that the way things were left between us would leave you a little cold but-"

I whipped my head around, holding his gaze. "A little cold? You knew how vulnerable I was. You knew how I felt about you. And you left without so much as a note!" I had tried to keep my mouth shut, but it wasn't really in my nature. And besides, if I didn't nip this in the bud he'd probably continue to try to win me over. But I was un-winnable.

He put one hand up in defense. "Jen, I was sixteen. I had no control over what happened after your mother found out."

"Found out what? What are you talking about?"

There was a moment of hesitation before he clarified. "She found out about us and she fired my mother and told us to get out or she was going to call the FBI and have my mother deported." The shock must have been clear on my face. He put a strong but gentle hand on my lower back and tried to pull me against him.

I shook my head as I pushed away from him and moved to the other side of the elevator. "No. She wouldn't do that." The elevator opened and I stalked out of it. Something wasn't right about that story. My mother knew how I'd felt about Dominic. I'd told her about him from the very start. And our relationship had gone on for a good nine months before he'd left. If she had wanted me to stay away from him she would have said something long before that.

"Jen, wait." He was behind me, tugging on my elbow to stop me. "I wasn't there when it happened, but that's what my mother told me."

I paused again and turned around to face him, pulling my elbow free. "It doesn't matter, does it? You had my phone number. You had my email address. You knew where I lived. You could have called me or emailed me or written me a letter. But you didn't. I wasn't important enough to you." I felt the sting of tears in my eyes, but I blinked them back. I wasn't going to give him the satisfaction.

His face softened and he shook his head. "You're right, of course. I just didn't know what to say to you. I was afraid that I was going to get you into trouble if I wrote you a letter. And I didn't know where we were going. We moved down to Miami, Jen. I tried to get you out of my head but I couldn't. And when I turned eighteen I packed a bag and I went to find you. But you weren't there. You'd moved."

I chuckled and shrugged my shoulders. "Great timing. A believable lie."

His face hardened. "It's not a lie."

I shrugged again. "Whatever you say, Dominic. Just like always."

He ran a hand through his neatly-trimmed black hair in exasperation. "We were kids. I had very little control over anything. But I'm a man now. And you are a woman. We can say and do whatever we want." He searched my eyes and then looked away. "I'm sorry." His gaze locked on mine again and I felt my breath catch in my throat. His eyes were so serious, so filled with desire. Still. After all these years. And I felt it too. "I can't take back the past. I was a stupid boy when you last saw me. But I'm all grown up now. I know how to treat a woman. Let me show you."

I was frozen in place. I wasn't sure what to say. Did I let him show me? How was he going to show me? My mind was so filled with lust I couldn't see past it. I needed to get away from him so I could clear my head and think rationally. I may have still felt something for Dominic Santos, but that didn't mean I needed to act on it.

"I have to go." Before my feet could move his hand was sliding through my blonde hair, holding my head in place, and his lips met mine. With eyes open he kissed me. It was the most erotic moment in my life. He was seeing me. Kissing me. Before I could get lost in it he pulled away, stroking my cheek twice with his thumb before letting me go.

Good night was all he said before he turned and headed back to the elevator, leaving me reeling and confused. And really horny.

Chapter 4

I drove around aimlessly for twenty minutes before I finally decided that the only thing I needed to calm me down was a little shopping therapy. It had always worked in the past. It was something I'd been taught by my mother. When you're feeling out of control just pop on down to Neiman Marcus and take back the control.

I felt the tension leaving my body as soon as I stepped into the store. Everything about it, from the smell of new leather mixed with designer perfume to the hundreds of lights sprinkled on the ceilings, soothed me almost instantly. As was customary for me I started in the shoe department. After informing the salesman that I was just browsing, I did just that. I let my eyes and fingers roam over the various styles, textures and colors. I picked up at least half a dozen, getting a feel for them in my slender hands.

After leaving the shoe department I moved on to the clothing department. The store had been decorated for the holidays for weeks now but I was still enchanted with their elegant decorations. Twinkling lights mingled with fresh greenery and ribbons of red. Everywhere you looked there were gentle reminders that it was the Christmas season.

I turned my eyes back to the task at hand and moved over to the dresses. Since my coffee stain dress was ruined I figured I'd go ahead and find myself a replacement. I flipped through the clothes slowly, methodically. With each pause I quickly assessed how the garment would lie on my body. I was not an easy body type to shop for. My hips were slightly flared, my legs were long and my chest was too busty to fit in a lot of styles that were currently popular.

My fingers paused when I glanced up and my eyes landed on a black on nude Rachel Gilbert dress that was illuminated with a spotlight from the heavens. The saleswoman must have seen both a hefty commission check and an enamored buyer because she was at my side, trying to guess my dress size before I stopped in front of the dress. Oh, it was glorious. I told her my size and she fished it down and held it with care as she moved towards the dressing rooms.

When she left I made slow work of undressing. The anticipation of what was to come was too exciting to rush. I carefully slipped the dress from the hanger and gently tugged it on. Already I loved the way it looked but it needed to be zipped for the full effect. With my hands pressed to my chest to keep the dress in place I tiptoed out of the fitting room.

"I'm looking for something for a woman."

I paused and held my breath as his voice washed over me. Dominic. What was he doing here? Shopping for a woman? I ignored the burn of jealousy as it singed my guts. I could care less who he was shopping for. He was a no good liar. I'd had my fill of those.

I was torn between interrupting Dominic's shopping trip to get the sales woman's attention and turning around and getting out of my safe-place which was suddenly infiltrated by the enemy and was no longer safe. After a few seconds debate I decided on the former. Let him wait like I'd waited for him all those years ago. And longer. It had taken me a long time to let go of the idea that Dominic was going to come back and beg my forgiveness. I'd tried to drown myself in men and bad situations so he'd come rescue me. Then I grew up and realized I was only hurting myself.

I cleared my throat loudly, drawing both pairs of eyes towards me. "Excuse me, could you assist me with my dress?"

Before the sales woman could respond Dominic was on his way over. I frowned at him and pointed to the open-mouthed older woman slowly approaching us. "I was talking to her."⊠"Maybe so, but nonetheless I would be more than happy to help you."

"I don't need or want your help, Dr. Santos."

He feigned a wounded expression. "Mi amore, you wound me."

"Payback is a bitch," I said and then glanced over his shoulder with a courteous smile, signaling silently that I still required her help.

"You look stunning in that dress," he whispered huskily, moving in closer.

I waved my hand to the sales woman as I took a step back, his words ruffling me. "No, nevermind. I have changed my mind. This is definitely not the dress for me. Thank you." I returned his amused grin with an annoyed glare before returning to my dressing room. As I was shutting the door I caught his gaze leering at my exposed back. I shut the door loudly and counted to ten in my head.

I wasn't going to let him get to me. I could do this. I was strong. I undressed and left the dress draped across the chair. I was even more mad at him now that he'd ruined another beautiful dress for me. I took a long time in the dressing room, patting down my hair and smoothing out wrinkles that weren't there, hoping that when I came out he would be gone.

Apparently, it was not my lucky day.

I kept my chin high as I walked past him but he followed, falling into step beside me as we exited the lady's clothing section.

"Funny thing running into you twice in one day. Perhaps fate is finally on our side," he said, a slight chuckle mingling with his words.

"No. You're mistaken. This is karma." Why wouldn't he take the hint and leave me alone? He'd done a fine job of it in the past.

"Do you believe in karma?" he asked, his hands stuffed into his pockets. I felt my body tingle in delight every time his elbow brushed against my arm.

"I don't believe in anything, Dr. Santos, except the power of the all mighty dollar. Speaking of the all mighty dollar, I do believe you're going to be overseeing my work. I'd appreciate it if we could meet next week, if you aren't too busy, which my father has assured me that you aren't, so that you can approve my plans. Or we could just skip all that formal stuff and I'll just go ahead with the planning, and you can lie and say you looked it all over. I'm sure it would bore you to tears anyway."

My interests had always bored my ex-husband, Kent, to tears. No matter how many times I'd tried to get him interested in what I cared about, it always failed. It was better now that we were divorced and I was rid of him, but I just wished it hadn't stolen so many years of my life. I'd sacrificed so much for him, but namely my career.

"I helped with planning several of the charity events while I was in Miami," he said, interrupting my thoughts. "Perhaps I could even be helpful to you."

I stole a sideways glance at him, surprised. "Really? How many guests?"

He shrugged his broad shoulders. "Depended on the event. They ranged from five-hundred to five-thousand."

"Impressive. Why did you do it? To meet women?" I watched him carefully. If he did do it to meet women I wouldn't be surprised. That's the only reason I could think of for a man like Dominic, a man like my father, to engage in any part of planning a charity event.

He laughed softly before his expression turned slightly somber as we stepped out into the parking lot, the sky quickly darkening above us. "No. I did it for my mother. She died of breast cancer and it's a small way for me to honor her, to host and plan galas for the Susan Komen Foundation."

I felt a small tug in my chest for his pain. I pressed my lips together as my eyes dropped to my hands which were clutching my Coach purse tightly. Speaking of death always made me uncomfortable. I hadn't experienced that kind of loss in my life. I was lucky. "I'm sorry," I said. I meant it. His mother had been a nice woman. Always so kind and warm. She'd bake me cookies every day and they'd be waiting for me on the counter when I returned from school. Until my mother told her to stop, that is, because she said I was getting too chunky.

"I'm sure she is in heaven, waiting for me." When I glanced up he winked at me, a smile on his lips that put me at ease. No doubt it did the same for most people, especially the female ones. "It was a hard time in my life, for sure. And I still miss her. But that's why I do it. If you don't already have plans, we could have dinner tonight and talk about the plans for the gala?"⊠I scoffed, "No, I don't want your name anywhere near the gala planning. I don't want you taking credit for my hard work."

"Perhaps you can take the credit for my hard work."

I didn't know how he managed to make everything sound so sexual. Perhaps it was just me being a crazy, delusional, sex-starved woman. I gripped my purse tightly to remind me to calm down before shaking my head. "No. I'd better get home and start finalizing the plans for our meeting first thing Monday morning."

He didn't seem at all surprised or angry that I'd just penciled myself into his work calendar. "Nine?"

We stopped at the rear of my car and I finally met his gaze again. I saw something soft there but I was determined to ignore it. We were business acquaintances now. We had to remain professional. "See you then," I said with a nod and a polite smile before climbing into my car.

I wasn't about to lose this job for some man. I'd already been there and done that. I'd already been there and done that with Dominic, too. I reminded myself that it was a much younger Dominic but that only made thinking about him worse. I wondered how he'd matured since the last time I'd seen him. His voice had certainly changed for the better and his body was much more defined and filled out than it had been in his youth. I shook my head and switched the heat off. With the cold air blasting in my face, I felt my heart rate return to normal. Unfortunately, Dominic continued to be on my mind for the rest of the evening.

Chapter 5

The weekend was long. Too long. And I hated to admit that I was very much looking forward to my meeting with Dominic this morning. I wanted to say that the mere thought of his face made me vomit in my mouth a little, however, that was as far from the truth as one could get.

I'd taken great pains this morning to get my blonde hair into a romantic knot at the base of my head. I made sure my makeup was enough to cover my flaws but not enough to make it look unnatural. And I put on my hottest work-appropriate dress, which as it happened also doubled to be the most erotic. It was made of bonded lambskin and felt incredible to the touch. At first sight I wanted to touch it, part of me hoped Dominic felt the same way when he saw me in it.

If he was going to come back into my life I was going to make it my mission to torture him as payback for the wrongs he'd done to me in my youth. And for ruining me for other men and preventing me from finding true love, if such a thing actually existed. If he hadn't fucked me up so badly I probably would have no doubt of its existence.

My Christian Louboutin black spike covered pumps clicked gleefully as I walked the hall towards Dominic's office. I smiled as his secretary's eyes popped open at my appearance. I could only hope he'd have the same reaction.

As I turned to go into his office I stopped short, the smile falling from my lips. Dominic was sitting, a charming smile on his lips as he stared up at Kelly, who sat on the corner of his desk, long legs crossed, exposed by the short skirt she'd decided to wear.

I cleared my throat loudly as I knocked on his still open door. At the noise they both turned, their smiles slowly dropping.

"Well, I'd better get going before Dr. Derby discovers that I'm missing," Kelly said as she hopped off Dominic's desk and made her way towards me. She shot me an innocent smile as she squeezed past and left us alone. My eyes turned back to Dominic and I raised my eyebrows in question.

"Can't stand up when a lady enters the room? You know my father looks down on fraternization between his staff."

His dark eyes roamed over my body slowly, taking in every inch of my dress. They seemed to stare directly at my nipples which were hardening by the second.

"I just need a moment." He dropped his eyes to his desk and shifted in his seat, one hand disappearing under the desk.

I rolled my eyes. "Would you like me to close the door and come back in five minutes so you can get a hold of yourself?" I felt the jealousy biting at me thinking of him having an erection because of Kelly.

His eyes came back to me along with a pained smile. "No, come in, sit down." I was about to close the door when his words stopped me. "No, please, leave it open." Why on earth would he want the door open during our meeting? Was he hoping that Kelly would walk by and see us chatting and get jealous? Or was he trying to avoid having others thinking that we might be doing something less than decent in his office? It didn't matter either way I reminded myself, as I went to sit down. I pulled the file folder from my bag and held it out to him. He took it and placed it on top of his empty desk.

"How was your weekend?" he asked, his eyes down on the papers. He was avoiding looking at me. Perhaps he was put off by the scowl on my face. My mood was still sour by what I'd walked in on.

"It was wonderful. Wonderful and full of sex," I lied. I don't know why I lied. No, I did know. I wanted him jealous. I wanted to torture him. That was my mission.

He continued to look at the papers, unphased by my admission. "That's wonderful for you." He paused when he came to the gala cost estimation. Slowly his finger slid down the row of figures. He tapped the total a couple of times. "Dr. Derby said we need to keep costs low. This is forty percent more than what he had budgeted for."

I scoffed as I leaned forward to look at the figure. "There is nothing I can do to lower that short of cutting the number of guests and then we won't meet the charity goal for the year."

"I'll have to think of this for a little while. Can you come back at the end of the day? I should have a solution by then." Finally his dark-chocolate-colored eyes raised and gazed directly into mine. I felt my core heat. I wasn't sure why, there was nothing particularly carnal in his gaze. He seemed to be all business.

"Fine. Perhaps I'll have a solution too." I reached for my papers but his hand clamped down on the file. "What are you doing?" I demanded.

"I need this to look over in more depth. I'll hand it back this evening."

I drew my hand back and stood up, keeping the staring contest between us going strong. "Fine. Have a wonderful day, Dr. Santos. I do hope Kelly will come back to keep you entertained further."

I turned on my heel and started out of his office, just as I reached the door he spoke again. "Mrs. Little, could you please shut the door on your way out?" I ground my teeth together in irritation at his request.

Just before I slammed it closed I called over my shoulder, "Don't rub it too hard or you'll chafe."

Chapter 6

"Jen, are you alright, darling? You seem very distracted." My mother's hand on mine brought me back to the present. I'd joined my mom for lunch at the country club, the one I'd been putting off with her for a few days. Not intentionally, of course, but the gala had consumed me since Daddy had told me I'd be overseen by Dominic Santos.

Dominic. It was time to share with my best friend, my mother, about what had been distracting me. I took a sip of my bubbly, pale prosecco before speaking up, "Daddy hired a new doctor at the firm."

"Oh?" My mother stabbed a tender piece of lettuce and brought it towards her mouth.

"Dominic Santos."

My mother started coughing at the mere mention of his name, her eyes dropping to her water and then her plate when she brought the water to her lips to clear the clog in her throat.

Strange. "Do you remember him?"

"Hmm?" She met my gaze with raised eyebrows, playing coy but I knew she was anything but.

"The boy I fell in love with when I was in high school. The boy who disappeared practically overnight. You know what he told me? He said that you threatened to have his mother deported because he was seeing me."

She laughed softly and shook her head. "Jen. Listen, I did do that, and I'm not proud, but it wasn't me who found out, it was your father. He always made me do all his dirty work."

I frowned as I digested that information. She had always been the one barking orders around the house, even to my father, on the few rare occasions that he was home. "I see. Why didn't you tell me? Why did you let me believe that he didn't love me and just left?" She continued to eat, I could see in the drop of her shoulders that she was feeling relief. "Jen, what could I say to my fourteen year old daughter? You were a teenager, if I had told you the truth you would have run after him. It was the only thing I could do that would keep you safe. And now that you're older I'm sure you understand that it wasn't real love. It was puppy love. Your teenage crush." She put her fork down and cocked her head to the side. "You do understand that, don't you?"

I picked at the salad still on my plate, avoiding her eyes. Did I? I had no idea what I understood anymore. Ever since he'd come back my mind and body had been out of sync with each other. I took another sip of the wine, hoping it would hurry up and give me a little buzz so I wouldn't have to think while sober. I didn't want to accept that my mother had lied to me. I thought we told each other everything. I thought she was the one person who I could trust.

"He's grown into a very handsome man," I said, testing the truth waters.

"I'm sure he is, darling, he was a good looking boy when he was younger, too. But looks aren't everything. You need to keep your eye on your future, darling. Oh, I've booked us a two-week cruise to the Bahamas."

"You've already booked it?"

"Yes, I was sitting at my desk when an ad popped up and I clicked it and had to book it immediately. We're going to have the most fabulous New Year's this year, Jen. Two good looking single women, ready to turn heads and break hearts." She smiled and I felt my stomach do an angry flip.

She knew that the gala was important to me. She knew my job was important to me, so why did she schedule a two-week cruise for us right around the gala? I would be swamped with all the details and follow through.

She reached out across the table and grabbed ahold of my hand, squeezing it gently as she met my eyes, a smile in hers. "Don't worry, darling, I already cleared it with your father."

I pulled my hand away and grabbed the napkin that was in my lap, setting it on the table next to my plate. "Mom, I can't go on a cruise. You shouldn't have run it by daddy, you should have asked me."

She frowned as she pulled back her hand. "Jen, honestly, I don't see what the big deal is. You'll get someone else to handle those last minute details. Someone like Kelly."

Kelly. The mention of her name caused the morning to flash through my memory. Her on Dominic's desk, him smiling and refusing to stand when I entered his office. Him probably jerking himself off under his desk after I left all because of her.

"Mom, I have to go. I have some work to do. Work. Because I do that."

She looked offended. "Jen, I made sure you got the best divorce attorney so you wouldn't have to work. You can live the life of leisure, be pampered, go see the world."

With a sinking feeling in my gut I realized that despite how much I loved my mother I didn't want to end up like her. I didn't want to be rich and alone. I wanted to find someone to share my life with. ⊠"I love you, Mom. I'll see you next week." I hugged her after she stood and started to walk away.

"Stay away from him, Jen."

I let her words resonate in my head as I left the restaurant. I hadn't had any intention of going near him. She had nothing to worry about.

Chapter 7

Dominic had texted me just after lunch to tell me he was running behind schedule and asked me to stop by the office around six. He apologized but I knew he hadn't really meant it.

I knocked on his office door, glancing around the nearly empty office setting as I waited for him to open it. For a moment I thought perhaps he'd duped me and had already gone home for the night. The door opened and Dominic stood there, as soon as his office air hit me I felt my knees weaken. His scent had filled the room, his cologne was a mixture of male skin and leather and sandalwood. I reminded myself to stay strong as his handsome smile accosted me.

"Jen. Thanks for coming in so late. I hope I didn't ruin your plans for the evening."

I scoffed as I quickly took him in. He was wearing a white button down shirt tucked into pair of gray Armani slacks. "I'm sure that's not true. I'm sure that was what you were hoping to do."

He stepped back and waved a hand towards the empty chair I'd sat in earlier. "Come in, we'll discuss the gala."

I stepped in and felt tingles on my skin as I heard the door click behind me. I made the mistake of turning around and meeting his gaze. It was heated and the lighting was dim, the only real light coming from a lamp on his desk. My breath caught in my throat as his fingers tickled the inside of my wrist. A questioning touch. I quickly pulled my hand away and sat down.

"Did you find a solution to the budget problem?" I asked, suddenly feeling very much like a mouse in the lion's den. I crossed my legs and set my hands carefully on the arms of the chair to reaffirm my position. I was in control. It was how I liked it. Always.

He cleared his throat before moving around his desk and resumed his seated position. He scratched at the back of his dark hair for a moment. "Yes."

I offered him a quizzical look.

He cleared his throat once more. "The open bar can be cut. Make it a cash bar, charging a little more than the caterer's rates, and all extra profits from it can go towards the charity. We can opt for something other than fresh flowers on the tables. Flowers in the winter are too expensive. Go with some fresh holly or something else that's in season."

I nodded. "Those all seem reasonable. I had already decided against the flowers, as well. Is that all?"

His eyes roamed over my face for a long moment before he licked his lips and sat back in his chair. He gave me a slight nod. "Yes, that's all."

"That wasn't so bad, was it? I don't know why we couldn't have discussed this some other time. I don't know why it had to be so late into the evening when every one else gets to leave and enjoy themselves." I reached for my file and was about to pull it towards myself when his hand reached out and held onto mine.

I stared at his hand for a long moment as the heat flooded my body.

"Jen."

I forced myself to remember that very morning, dousing myself with a dose of a reality. "Dominic."

"The next time you come into the office you need to wear something more appropriate for an office environment."

I pulled my hand back roughly. "Excuse me?"

"It was all I could do to control myself this morning when you walked into my office wearing… that dress."

I felt a smile curl on my lips as I watched his eyes heat. "Is that so? You liked my dress?"

He shook his head in a disapproving manner. "Was that your intent? To make me notice you? You didn't need a dress to do that."

"Why would I want to do that? I've already told you, I have no interest in you."

It was his turn to smile. "You have not said as much, but now I know for sure you aren't interested. Kelly will be glad to hear it. I had mentioned I was unavailable but now that I know we have no chance…" He paused and assessed my face which felt very much like it was being pinched in a vice. "Is something wrong, Jen?"

"No, what would possibly be wrong?"

"I don't know. You just suddenly look very angry. Did something I said upset you?" Damn him, he was still smiling at me.

"I told you how my father feels about fraternization."

"Oh, that, yes, well, it was a stipulation when coming to work for him."

I frowned. "A stipulation? You put in writing that you could sleep with and kiss whomever you wanted at my father's practice?"

He shrugged one shoulder casually, the smile mocking me. "What can I say, Jen? He told me that you were working for him and I thought maybe you'd give me a chance. Obviously I was mistaken."

"Obviously." I held my hand out for my folder, keeping my nose poised high in the air. He could date Kelly and whomever else he wanted for all I cared. It was probably time for me to spread my professional wings anyhow. I didn't want to stay under the employ of my father forever.

He made no move to hand the folder back to me. "How long are we going to play this game?"

I snatched the folder up and stood. "I wasn't aware that we were playing a game."

He chuckled. "Come on, Jen. I'll play for as long as you'd like, you're worth waiting for, but I'd rather not. I'd rather skip all of this back and forth and get to the part where we are admitting that we have feelings for each other. I want to take you places you haven't ever been before. I want to congratulate you on all the big things you're going to be doing in your life now that you're out on your own."

"You want to tie me down and cage me, you mean?"

A look of confusion passed over his face. "No? Jen, I don't know who you think I am but--"

"I think you're the guy who left me without a fight. That's who I think you are. And I think when the time comes you'll do it again. Goodnight, Dominic."

Chapter 8

I reached into my purse for my keys and frantically searched for them. It was getting darker and for some reason my body was on edge. I glanced around to see if anyone else was watching and I saw no one. I did see a dark colored mini cooper parked near the back of the garage. Probably Dominic's.

With a groan I turned back and headed upstairs to the offices again. I must have forgotten my keys or dropped them somewhere along the way. The elevator doors slid open and as I stepped out I heard voices carrying down the dimly lit hallways. I paused and strained to listen. One of them was definitely Dominic's and the other was also familiar. Female. I removed my heels as my heart hammered in my chest. Ignoring the disgust I felt at walking with bare feet on a public floor I crept through the hallways, growing closer to Dominic's door until the voices cleared and I could hear clearly.

"...none of your business, Mrs. Derby."☒"This is very much my business. This is my daughter we're talking about. How can you possibly make her happy?"

"In case you haven't noticed I'm successful."

"Success isn't everything. It doesn't make a man a good husband I should know I--"

"You were married to one. And he cheated on you. I know. My mother told me, she told me the real reason why you sent us away."

"Can you blame me? How could I have her living anywhere near my family. She was going to ruin my reputation and destroy my life!"

For a few moments I felt my heart freeze in my chest. I put my hand to my mouth as I continued to listen, unable to move or speak. I was… shocked at what I was hearing.

"I've kept your secret, Mrs. Derby. I didn't want to destroy your family and I didn't want you to take my mother away from me. But she's gone now, in heaven, and you're no longer married to him. You will not continue to stand in the way of Jen's happiness. I'm not afraid of you anymore."

My mother scoffed. "Jen is a good girl, she'll do whatever I suggest to her. I suggested she marry Kent, she did. I suggested she play homemaker instead of getting a job so that when they finally divorced she would have some security. She did that as well. I just wanted to let you know that your efforts to try to win her over won't get you anywhere. I'll poison you to her. I've already started."

Somewhere inside I felt my insides crumble. All this time I thought my father was the one I should be afraid of. I thought he was the bad guy because he couldn't stay faithful to my mother. But he just didn't love her anymore. And he was lonely because she… she was manipulative and spiteful. And she obviously didn't love me. How could she love me when she was trying to prevent me from finding happiness? Not that Dominic was certain to be my happiness but…perhaps he was? He certainly had been in the past. Before she ripped him away from me to save her own humility.

I came forward finally, Dominic's eyes finding me as soon as I showed up in his doorway, his hands were tucked in his pockets. He looked fierce and sexy as hell standing up for me to my mother.

"Kelly? Was that your poison?" It was all clicking into place. All these tiny little things that had happened in my life. She always said it would be a certain way and it was. I began to wonder how much of my life was without her hand in it.

She turned around and put a hand to her chest. "Jen. My goodness, you scared me. I was just coming by to see the new doctor you mentioned at lunch."

"Mom, please. Don't insult me." I felt the tears in my eyes as I stared at her feign innocence. I'd learned that look from her.

"Let's not get emotional, Jen." She pulled a handkerchief from her purse and held it out, reaching for my eyes.

I pushed her hand away and turned my face. "Don't. Don't try to fix me, mother. Nothing is wrong with me. People cry. Normal people cry. I can't believe you'd do that to me. I can't believe you'd rip up my heart to save your reputation. How can you be so … selfish?"

She stuffed the handkerchief back into her purse and shrugged her shoulders. "One day you'll understand why I did it, Jen. Apparently not to-day. Sit with it for a week or two and think about it. Think what you would do if you were in my shoes. What would you do if Kent were sleeping with the help? Would you just let it happen? Suffer social suicide with a divorce knowing that he'd bring her into the house to take your place? A maid?" She shook her head as she tucked her purse under her arm. "I did what I had to do."

"Get out," Dominic snapped, "or I will call security. And unless you have an appointment don't come back into this building. Not while I'm still employed here." She laughed, "What do you think my husband will say about you speaking to me this way?"

"Your ex-husband," I said, driving the nail into her quickly closing coffin. "He would agree, mother, and you know it. Leave."

"Fine. Come along, Jen, I found your keys on the floor on the way in. I'll walk you to your car."

I grabbed the keys that were dangling from her fingers and stepped over towards Dominic. As I grew closer his hand moved to my lower back. He was on my side. It felt so good to have someone on my side. Finally. Once again.

My mother rolled her eyes and sighed. "So dramatic. Fine. I'll see you next week for lunch. Goodnight." Without a look back or even the semblance that she'd done anything remotely wrong she walked away.

When we heard the gentle tremor of the elevator doors closing I stepped away, gently wiping at my eyes. My body already missed his presence.

I sniffled softly and then met his eyes, offering him a small smile. "Thanks for backing me up."

"Jen, I'm sorry that I didn't tell you the truth about your moth-"

I held up a hand to stop him. "I forgive you. I forgive you for running away. I forgive you for not coming back for me. I wouldn't want to be involved with me either. Not after knowing that I came from that." I waved a hand over my shoulder to the door where my mother had recently departed from.

"That isn't why. I was still afraid that she would take my mother away from me, Jen. It had nothing to do with you. Not like now. I'm here now because of you. All I'm asking for is one more chance."

I swallowed hard as I met his eyes. He stepped forward and gently put his hands on my arms. His hands were so warm and strong.

"Please," he whispered as he stepped in closer to my body until we were flush together from chest to thighs. My resolve was quickly melting. My mind reeling for a reason why I shouldn't. He hadn't run away because he'd wanted to and he hadn't stayed away because he'd wanted to. He'd stay away for the love of his mother, may she rest in peace.

I had done some terrible things, I had slept around and cheated, lashing out at innocent people, just like my mother had. I was angry. Angry at him for leaving me. Angry at my parents for not making their marriage work. Angry at myself for not being good enough to make either of them happy. But it was all misplaced. Perhaps he wouldn't love me once he knew all of those things. Or perhaps he would. I was going to give him a chance to discover them all and decide for himself.

I closed my eyes tightly and tried to fight the urges that were bursting inside of me but I couldn't.

His fingers combed through my hair until my head was tilted back and then he brought his lips to my exposed throat. My fists were curled in my lap as my eyes closed, savoring the feelings he brought out of me.

"Dominic…" the whisper from my throat sounded foreign to my ears.

"Si, mi amor," his breath tickled my neck as he responded and moved to cover more of my flesh with his lips. I felt the familiar heat between my legs as his scruff scraped against my skin, an intoxicating contrast to his soft sensual lips. "Do you want me to stop?"

I shook my head as my hands reached up and grabbed onto the back of his neck. I brought my lips to his and held him there, kissing him until we were both breathless and needy. With ease he slipped his hands beneath me and lifted me. As we kissed I heard the crash of his desk's contents hit the floor. He laid me on my back and ran his hand up the length of my thigh, pushing my dress further up for access. I groaned against his mouth as his thick fingers found my center. I groaned as his finger slipped between my panties. "Dominic!" His name was a hiss of pleasure as his finger slid with ease inside of me. He was testing the waters and they were flooded. He pulled away from my mouth for a moment. I gasped in pleasure as he took his finger coated with my juices into his mouth, sucking them off.

His eyes were darker now, his desire showing there and in other places. I allowed my eyes to drift lower and felt more wetness flooding me at the sight of his arousal straining against his navy blue trousers. He hooked his fingers into my panties and quickly slid them off, tossing them aside as I reached for his pants and undid them. I wanted him like I'd only dreamt of wanting someone before. Again I was reminded of our teenage years -- me ready and willing to be taken, him teasing me, building me up, but not ready to take me. He'd wanted to wait then. I hoped he had no intention of waiting now. We were adults. Two consenting, I hoped, adults. I waited for him to stop me from pushing his pants down but he didn't.

He slid his hands down my thighs, hooking his fingers behind my knees and spread me wide for him. I fell back onto the desk as I put my hands on his forearms, feeling the power beneath my hands. He grabbed ahold of himself and slowly slid into me. His hand moved behind my back and I was once again lifted. I wrapped my arms and legs around him, my lips parted slightly as I stared into his intense gaze.

With a grunt he held on tight and thrust himself into me. I felt my cheeks heat. Never before had I been so possessed by a man. We stared at each other, lost in each other as he did it again and again. He filled me forcefully, arousing every part of my body and my mind. When his lips crashed down onto mine again he moved us towards the wall. With my back firmly in place he eased his grip around me and started to go slower. I continued to kiss him as we rose in heat together. He had tried to hold back but soon he was thrusting quickly inside of me. And then we were both lost, hands over each other's mouth to hold back the sounds of release.

"That was worth the wait," he murmured against my lips just before kissing them again.

It was.

* * *

Thanks for reading! If you want to stay in the loop be sure to sign up for my newsletter by going to my website: www.mariecolebooks.com As a thank you for subscribing I'll send you a copy of HS Friends [Elly and Kent's high school experiences] absolutely free! You've got nothing to lose.

PS - Please don't forget to tell
me what you thought about
the series on Amazon and
Goodreads.